The Boo Ghost Dance

Written by Tom Christopher

Illustrated by Heather Reilly

Published by Reilly Books
At Createspace
www.reillybooks.com

ISBN: **978-1-989597-01-9**

This book is dedicated to all the children who get to go trick or treating, and to those who might not get to this year. We wish them a safe and happy Halloween!

This book is also dedicated with love to Poppy Dave and Nanny Theresa's beautiful grandchildren: Logan, Lyla, Kacie, and Colin.

There's an old abandoned house

Sitting high upon a hill.

It's a very spooky place,

Empty, dark, and still.

The Boo Ghosts throw a party

Every Halloween they do.

The guests come from all over

To dance the whole night through.

Mr. Skeleton with his top hat

Greeting guests at the door,

His bones are all a rattling

When he's out on the dance floor.

Here comes Mrs. Spider

With her legs of eight

Spinning webs as she arrives

She loves to decorate.

When the music starts to play

It's like they go into a trance,

They are out on the dance floor

Doing the Boo Ghost Dance.

Move your body to the left,

Move your body to the right,

Wave your arms in the air

Just like a bird in flight,

And do the Boo Ghost Dance,

Yes, do the Boo Ghost Dance.

Mr. Mummy says it's nice

To meet friends and unwind

All throughout the year

Feels like I'm in a bind.

Drippy Dracula looks great,

Tuxedo and bow tie,

When it's time for him to leave

Turn into a bat and he'll fly.

Zack the Zombie in the corner,

Looks like he's in a trance.

When the music starts to play

He will do the Boo Ghost Dance.

When the music starts to play

It's like they go into a trance,

They are out on the dance floor

Doing the Boo Ghost Dance.

Move your body to the left,

Move your body to the right,

Wave your arms in the air

Just like a bird in flight,

And do the Boo Ghost Dance,

Yes, do the Boo Ghost Dance.

Wiggles the Wandering Witch

Flies in on her broom,

Waving to them all

As she flies around the room.

When she's on the dance floor,

She needs some extra room.

When she does the Boo Ghost Dance,

She dances with her broom.

Scaredy the Cat walks across the floor,

A Boo Ghost screams in delight,

Scaredy is on the ceiling

Holding on with all his might.

Jack-O-Lantern grins and thinks:

Looks like all the guests are here.

Time for me to go around,

See how many I can scare!

A Boo Ghost sneaks behind him,

Blows out Jack-O-Lantern's light,

Laughs as he goes on his way,

"I think you just got a fright!"

Headless Hank is on the floor,

Holds his head in his hands,

Once he starts he can't stop

Doing the Boo Ghost Dance.

When the music starts to play

It's like they go into a trance,

They are out on the dance floor

Doing the Boo Ghost Dance.

Move your body to the left,

Move your body to the right,

Wave your arms in the air

Just like a bird in flight,

And do the Boo Ghost Dance,

Yes, do the Boo Ghost Dance.

Willy Warewolf says, "It's been a howl,

I have to say goodnight."

The night is almost over,

It's coming to daylight.

I'll see you all again next year

To give someone a fright.

We will dance the night away

Again on Halloween night.

About the Author & Illustrator

Albert (Tom) Christopher always had an interest in writing. He dabbled with poetry while living away in Ontario, but it wasn't until he returned to NL that he wrote his first song. Family encouraged him to record it, but he didn't sing or play any instruments. David J. Fitzpatrick from the Fables liked the song and recorded it. This is the beginning of DaNdA, a partnership that would go on to record four CDs to date. Tom paired up with author and illustrator Heather Reilly to bring the vision of his first Christmas book to life. Since then, they have collaborated on two more and now *An Old Time Christmas*, *Santa Really Does Know*, and *Santa Almost Missed Our Town* are enjoyed by young and old. Tom continues to write and is currently working on his fifth CD. He and Heather are now proud to present their fourth book The Boo Ghost Dance, a Halloween tale for the whole family. They hope you all welcome this book as enthusiastically as the last three.

Heather Reilly is the author and illustrator of storybooks and novels alike. A teacher by trade, she enjoys adding learning activities at the end of most of her storybooks. Her medieval fantasy novels in the *Binding of the Almatraek* series are enjoyed by teens and adults alike. The final book in the series *Warden's Warning* will be released later this year. Her work can also be found in Engen Book's *Fantasy From the Rock*, and *Flights From the Rock*. She is currently working on a new, adult dystopian novel that she hopes to release in 2022.